P9-DBM-103

# CORDUROY'S
# EASTER PARTY

Grosset & Dunlap

A bear's share of the royalties from the sale of
*Corduroy's Easter Party* goes to the Don and Lydia
Freeman Research Fund to support psychological
care and research concerning children with life-
threatening illness.

Some material in this book was first published in *Corduroy's Easter* in 1999 by Viking,
a division of Penguin Putnam Inc.

Text copyright © 2000 by Penguin Putnam Inc. Illustrations copyright © 1999, 2000 by
Lisa McCue. All rights reserved. Published by Grosset & Dunlap, a division of Penguin
Putnam Books for Young Readers, New York. GROSSET & DUNLAP is a trademark of
Penguin Putnam Inc. Published simultaneously in Canada. Printed in the U.S.A.

*Library of Congress Cataloging-in-Publication Data*

Corduroy's Easter party /illustrated by Lisa McCue.
    p. cm.
  Summary: As he and his friends get ready to celebrate Easter with a special party,
Corduroy wonders if the Easter Bunny is real.
    [1.Easter—Fiction. 2. Teddy bears—Fiction. 3. Toys—Fiction. 4. Parties—Fiction.]
  I. McCue, Lisa, ill. II. Grosset & Dunlap

PZ7.F8747 Cq 2000
[E]—dc21
                                                      99-53734

ISBN 978-0-448-42154-4       I J

# Corduroy's Easter Party

BASED ON THE CHARACTER CREATED BY DON FREEMAN

ILLUSTRATED BY LISA McCUE

Grosset & Dunlap, Publishers

It was the day before Easter, and Corduroy and his friends were at the playground. Puppy was having no luck getting his kite up in the air. But he didn't mind. Everyone was happy because tomorrow they were having an Easter party!

Dolly said, "I can't wait to see what the Easter Bunny brings us!"

The party was going to be at Corduroy's house. Mouse made a list of all the things they would need.

"Do you think the Easter Bunny likes jellybeans?" Mouse said.

"Don't forget to put down eggs," Dolly said. "We need lots to decorate for the Easter Bunny."

Corduroy didn't say anything. Everyone else had no doubt that the Easter Bunny was real. But deep down, Corduroy wasn't so sure. After all, nobody had ever *seen* the Easter Bunny.

Still, Corduroy didn't want to spoil the fun. He kept his doubts to himself.

By the time they were ready to go shopping, it was raining outside. So the friends put on their raincoats and their boots, and they brought their umbrellas. Mouse rode in the wagon. Rabbit caught raindrops on her tongue. Puppy jumped right in the middle of every single puddle. Ker-*splash*!

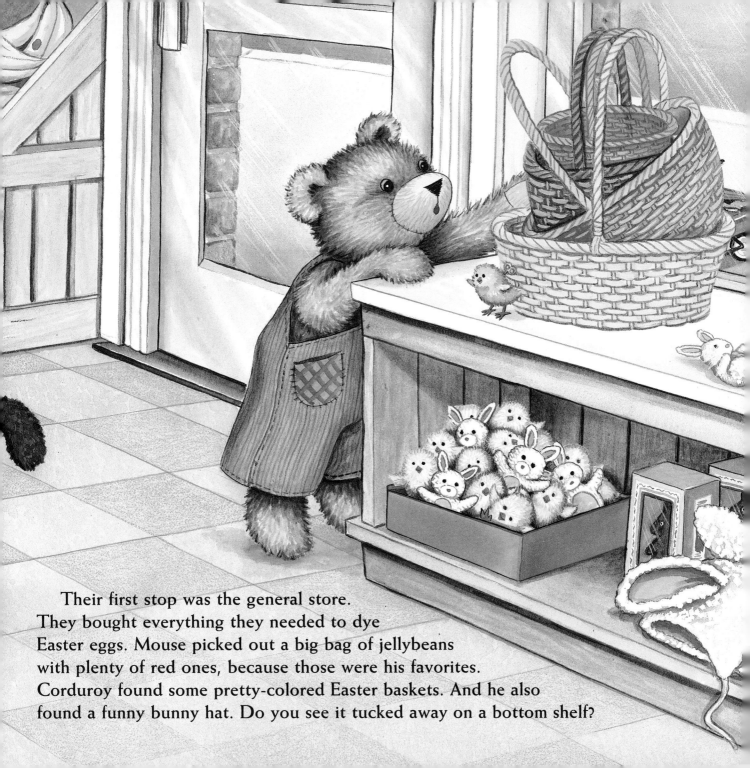

Their first stop was the general store.
They bought everything they needed to dye
Easter eggs. Mouse picked out a big bag of jellybeans
with plenty of red ones, because those were his favorites.
Corduroy found some pretty-colored Easter baskets. And he also
found a funny bunny hat. Do you see it tucked away on a bottom shelf?

"I am the Easter Bunny!" Corduroy said.

"No, silly," said Mouse. "The *real* Easter Bunny will be here tomorrow. But let's all get party hats." So they did. Dolly looked beautiful in her bonnet with flowers on the brim.

Puppy and Rabbit picked out very silly hats. Puppy's
looked like an Easter basket. Rabbit's had little chicks all
over it!

In a little while, the rain ended and the sun came out.
So Corduroy and his friends walked to their next stop—
the farm. They were having so much fun petting and saying
hello to the animals that they almost forgot why they came
—to buy eggs for decorating! Luckily, Dolly remembered!

Now did they have everything for their party? Not yet!
On their way home, the friends passed a meadow filled
with flowers. There were daffodils and tulips and daisies.

So they all picked little flower bouquets to use as decorations for the party. Corduroy could hardly wait to see how pretty his house was going to look!

Then Dolly and Rabbit hurried back to Corduroy's house with the party things. But Puppy was very thirsty from all the walking. So Corduroy and Mouse waited for him while he had a little drink.

Mouse lay back and daydreamed in the sun. "I'm so excited about Easter!" he said.

"Me too!" said Puppy.

Corduroy was, too. He *wanted* to believe in the Easter Bunny just like everybody else. But how could he know for sure?

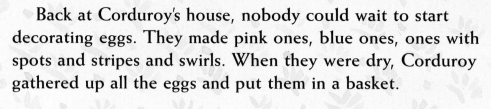

Back at Corduroy's house, nobody could wait to start decorating eggs. They made pink ones, blue ones, ones with spots and stripes and swirls. When they were dry, Corduroy gathered up all the eggs and put them in a basket.

It had been a very busy day. But now—
finally!—everything was ready for their
Easter party the next day.

It was the best party ever! They had cookies, and finger sandwiches cut into tiny triangles, and the most delicious fruit punch. Mouse ate so many red jellybeans he almost got a tummy ache!

Everybody wore their brand-new hats. Dolly looked
at Rabbit and giggled. "The chicks on your hat look so real,
I wouldn't be surprised if they started peeping!" she said.

And what was the perfect dance to do at an Easter party? Why, the bunny hop, of course! Corduroy led the way, with his bunny ears flopping as he hopped up and down. Rabbit was a natural at the bunny hop! Mouse got tired because his legs were shorter, but Dolly helped him keep up.

"Bunny hopping sure is good exercise!" said Mouse,
all out of breath.

Then it was time to go outside for the Easter egg hunt! Each of them hid a few eggs and then the hunt began. "Only one rule," said Corduroy. "No fair finding the eggs you hid yourself!" Corduroy peeked into the flowers. He saw some eggs, but they weren't the Easter kind! They were pretty blue robin's eggs!

After the hunt, everyone sat down on the grass and counted their eggs.

"What a perfect Easter!" said Dolly. "There's just one thing left."

"A visit from the Easter Bunny!" said Rabbit.

"When do you think he will come?" asked Mouse.

Corduroy did not know what to say. Easter was just about over. And still no sign of you-know-who.

But look! When Corduroy and his friends went back inside, there was a big surprise—a huge Easter basket filled with all kinds of candy! Can you guess who it was from?

Yes! It was from the Easter Bunny himself! He had come and gone while all the friends were outside. And he had even left them a note.

Have fun!
Your friend,
The Easter Bunny

As they sat around the table, eating the chocolate the Easter Bunny had left, Corduroy was so surprised, and so happy. "The Easter Bunny *is* real," he thought. Now he knew it for sure. And *that* was the best Easter surprise of all.

Happy Easter, everybody!